This Red
Wellies book
belongs to:

O Wen
Tomas
MacKenzie

for Peter and Emma

Look out for further illustrated stories about Felix the Fast Tractor
by Catherine Cannon

Why not visit www.felixthefasttractor.co.uk
for some fun colouring and games

Character illustrations by June Allan

First published in Great Britain by Red Wellies Publishing in 2004.

ISBN 0-9547701-1-0

Revised edition 2005.

Designed by Dene Marshall. Printed and bound by Reeds Printers, Penrith.

Felix the Fast Tractor
and the Coal Delivery

CATHERINE CANNON

Red Wellies Publishing

Felix the Fast Tractor lives on Ambers Farm with Farmer Story, Mrs Story, their two children Max and Lucy, and the family dog Ben.

It was wintertime and it had been snowing heavily for the past few days.

arm

Today was the first day that it hadn't snowed, and Daisy the Digger had come to help clear the snow from the farm lane.

5

Max and Lucy were busy making snowmen.
They were very excited as the village play
was that afternoon and they had been
practising their lines for weeks.

The bad weather had caused a big problem for Andrew the coalman as he was expecting an urgent delivery of coal to the train station. His coal bunkers were empty!

Felix and Daisy were on 'stand by' to help unload the coal and take it to Andrew's coal yard. But, at eleven o'clock, Andrew had telephoned to say that the coal trucks still couldn't get through to the train station.

The trucks were stuck ten miles away at the coal mine. Felix was worried that if the coal trucks couldn't get through, some people in the village wouldn't have any coal. So he started to think about what he could do to help.

Want to know more about the farm in winter?

During the winter months Farmer Story and Felix spend their time tidying up and spreading muck on the fields to make it good for growing. They also feed the animals, as there is less grass for them to eat in the winter.

Suddenly an idea came to him.

"Yes, that's it! With my snowploughs and the special 'train wheels' from the train station, I can go to the coal mine and bring the coal back to Andrew's yard!"

"What an excellent idea Felix," replied Farmer Story.

"I'll telephone Andrew, he will be delighted."

Andrew was waiting at the train station to help
fit the train wheels. The small metal wheels fitted
Felix perfectly and there was a big trailer that he
could use too.

"You'd better be quick," Andrew said to Felix. "The forecast is for snow this afternoon and we all need to be back for the village play, it starts at half past four."

Want to know more about train wheels?

Train wheels are a special attachment which fit onto machines like Felix to allow them to go on train tracks. They can be lowered when the vehicle has to run on the rails or raised to allow the vehicle to run on a road. Trailers can also have these special wheels.

It took a while to get the train wheels fixed on and it was one o'clock before Felix set off, clearing the deep snow as he went.

Want to know more about railways?

Railways are often used for carrying freight like coal, as the trains can pull many trucks a long way. Modern trains are powered by either diesel or electricity as they use less fuel than steam engines, which are powered by coal.

Felix was quite tired when he arrived at the mine, clearing the snow and pulling the big trailer was very hard work! The coal trucks were pleased to see him as they were still stuck in the deep snow in the rail sidings.

Felix positioned the trailer underneath the coal hopper and a big heap of coal was delivered into his trailer – along with a big cloud of coal dust! "Bye," he shouted to the trucks as he set off back to the train station.

Want to know more about coal?

Coal is a fuel which is found under the ground. It is known as a 'fossil' fuel because it was made millions of years ago from dead plants. It is mainly used for heating.

By this time it was three o'clock and it was starting to get dark. All of a sudden the sky turned very grey. "Oh no," thought Felix, "it's going to snow!" And snow it did. The snow started to settle on the train track, onto his bonnet and his windscreen. "Oh dear," he said to himself, "the village play starts soon and I've still got to get to the coal yard to unload the coal."

Felix arrived at the train station feeling very tired and very cold, but he knew he had to be as quick as he could. He lifted the train wheels and set off on the road back to the coal yard.

When Felix finally arrived at the coal yard it was four o'clock. He was very tired and very dirty. Daisy, Farmer Story and Andrew were all waiting for him.

20

"Thanks for all of your help Felix," Andrew said, "but with all of this new snow the roads are very slippery. There's no way I can get to the play, as the wheels on the coal wagon can't grip the roads in this weather. Everyone else has already left in the jeep."

Despite being tired and covered in coal dust and snow,
Felix knew he had to try to help.

"We could still make it in time," he said brightly.

He reversed up to the coal bunker and raised the trailer
as high as he could.

"Time to tip," he said, as all of the coal dropped out,
creating more clouds of black dust.

Andrew unhitched the trailer and jumped into Felix's cab and they set off through the thick snow. The coal dust on his windows and the blustery snow were making it difficult to see, and it was getting darker by the minute.

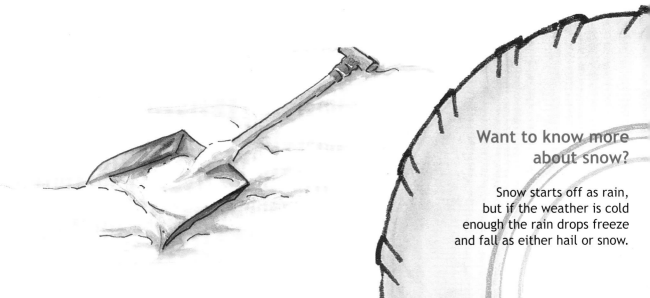

Want to know more about snow?

Snow starts off as rain, but if the weather is cold enough the rain drops freeze and fall as either hail or snow.

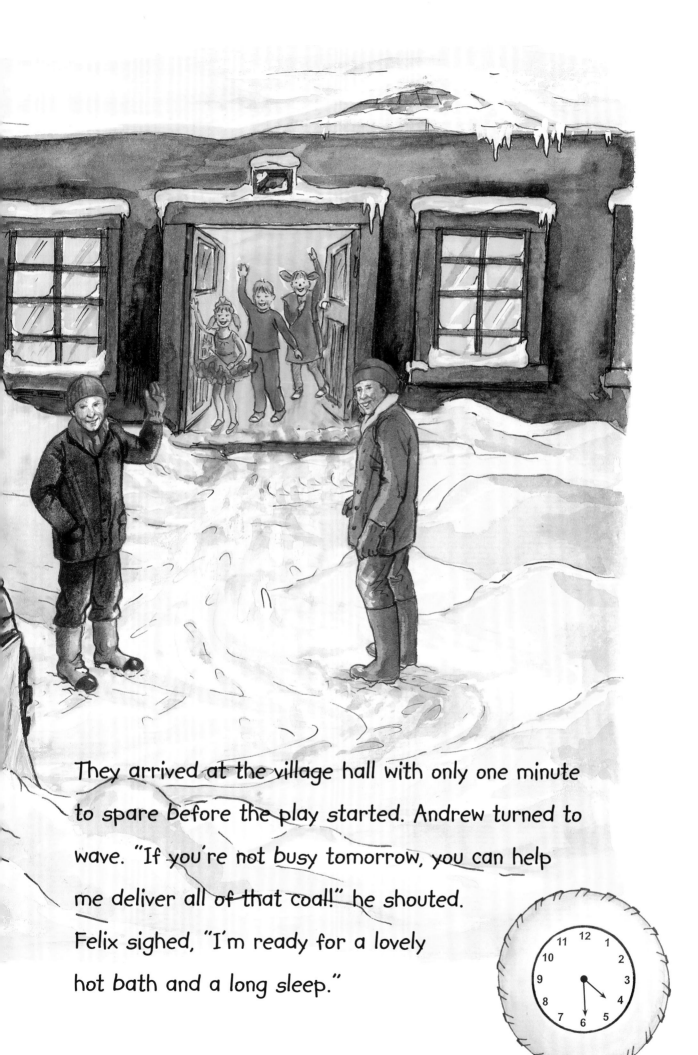

They arrived at the village hall with only one minute to spare before the play started. Andrew turned to wave. "If you're not busy tomorrow, you can help me deliver all of that coal!" he shouted.

Felix sighed, "I'm ready for a lovely hot bath and a long sleep."

lay

After the play Felix and Daisy were treated to bucketfuls of hot soapy water and a top-up of engine oil. "An excellent day's work you two," said Farmer Story. But he was talking to himself. Felix and Daisy had fallen fast asleep. He carefully pushed them into the cosy barn and tucked them in for the night. "Sleep tight," he whispered, as he quietly shut the barn door.

Rise and shine!

5am – Rise and shine, it's milking time! Farmer Story feeds the calves and cows and refreshes their bedding (straw and sawdust). The cows and calves stay inside during the winter months.

Follow Felix and Farmer Story on a typical winter's day at Ambers Farm.

9am (after breakfast) – Farmer Story and Felix go out into the fields to check on the sheep (shepherding). The sheep stay outside in the winter as they have warm woolly coats.

11am – There's always plenty to do on a farm and in the winter Farmer Story and Felix spend time mending fences, building walls and cutting hedges.

2pm – Felix puts a muck spreader on and goes around the fields spreading farm yard manure. The manure puts nutrients into the soil, making it ready for sowing in the spring.

4pm – The animals need feeding again, and the cows are milked before they go back to their beds.

7pm – It's dark, and Farmer Story has a final check on the animals before he closes Felix's door for the night – *sleep tight Felix!*

12.30pm (lunchtime) Farmer Story goes into the farmhouse for his lunch. He has some paperwork to do and some telephone calls to make – managing a farm involves more than just looking after the animals!

Sleep tight!

Also in this series:

Felix the Fast Tractor and the New Building

Follow Felix and his friends as they construct a new building on the farm – but what will it be used for? That's a secret!

Visit Felix and his friends on

www.felixthefasttractor.co.uk